THE TAL[illegible]G CAR

Also by Nicholas Fisk

MONSTER MAKER

THE TALKING CAR

Nicholas Fisk

Illustrated by Ann Johns

MAMMOTH

First published 1988 by
Macmillan Children's Books
Published 1990 by Mammoth
an imprint of Mandarin Paperbacks
Michelin House, 81 Fulham Road, London SW3 6RB
Reprinted 1990 (twice)

Mandarin is an imprint of the Octopus Publishing Group,
a division of Reed International Books Ltd.

ISBN 0 7497 0288 5

A CIP catalogue record for this title
is available from the British Library

Printed in Great Britain
by Cox & Wyman Ltd, Reading, Berkshire

THE TALKING CAR

'Oh, no, you don't!' Rob's father said.

'Please, Dad! Just once more!'

Because he'd seen his father trying to hide a smile, Rob leaned forward, switched off the ignition by turning the key one click, undid his seat belt and turned the key so that lights lit up on the fascia and the voice said,

'Kind–ly fast–en your seat belt!'

Rob giggled and his father's half-smile became a grin. 'Kind–ly fast–en your seat belt!' Rob said, imitating the car's voice. It was a young but ladylike, hooting voice, a bit muffled and tinny. It came from a little grille in the fascia.

'The motor can–not be start–ed until your seat belt is sec–ured,' said the car's voice, sounding prissier than ever.

'Bet I can start it,' Rob said. Before his father could stop him, he gave the key an extra, final twist. This should have operated the starter, but it did not: a little orange-red light appeared and something went *bleep–bleep–bleep*. Then the voice began repeating, *'The motor can–not be start–ed until—'*

'You shouldn't have done that,' Rob's father said angrily. 'You don't mess about with car keys. The engine might start with the car in gear. You're old enough to know that.'

'I'm only nine,' Rob said cheekily.

'Nine and a crafty little devil,' his father said. 'Seriously, Rob—'

'Sorry, Dad,' Rob said. And for the moment, he really was sorry. But only for the moment. This was the family's first really new car, straight from the showroom. There were so many things to look at and try out in it. Rob had bounced on the smart seats, held the steering wheel and made vroom-vroom noises, turned the lights on and off, opened the sun-roof, tried the gear-lever – everything.

But the voice was the best. 'It's terrific, great, magic, Dad!' Rob said. 'You were clever to choose this car!'

'Your mother chose it,' his father said. 'She liked the colour.'

'Do *you* like the colour, Dad?'

'Yes, it's all right.'

'I like the colour. And I like the seats and everything. But I like the voice best.'

'You would,' said his father.

'Why would I, Dad?'

'Because you never stop talking, just like the

car. Still, there's one good thing.'

'What's that?'

'You can turn the voice off. Like this, see? This little switch.'

'I like it turned on.' Rob leaned over and turned the voice on again.

The two of them sat in the car, staring at nothing. They were both quite happy. It's exciting just sitting in your new car. Every single thing is new, even the smell.

Then Rob touched all the switches and knobs, one after the other. 'Heater *up*, heater *down*, fan slower, faster, full blast—'

Rob's father said, 'I'm going to order another switch like the one that turns the voice off.'

'What for, Dad?'

'A switch for *you*!'

He grabbed his son by the throat. 'To silence you!' he said.

Rob laughed and choked and struggled to get free. He managed to get the car door open. At once the voice said, *'The front pass–en–ger's door is not shut, per–lease make sure all doors are sec–urely locked.'*

That made them both laugh. 'Teatime,' said Rob's father. They got out of the car, locked it up, made sure no lights were on and went to the house.

'It's a great car, Dad,' Rob said. 'But the voice is the best bit. It really is. Fancy us owning a new car that actually *talks*!'

After a week, the new car was still the new car, but now it was not quite so new. Rob's father had already found a few things to complain about at the dealer's. Rob's mother had broken a fingernail on the boot lid and called the new car some rude names. And the silvery, metallic finish of the new car was already a little dulled by road dirt.

Inside, however, the car seemed as new and exciting as ever to Rob. He sat in it for hours, sniffing the new smell, exploring all the new controls. As he was a sensible boy, his father and mother let him. '*Don't* turn on the lights because you'll drain the battery. Right?' said his father.

'Right,' replied Rob.

'And *don't* blow the horn or the neighbours will go mad and murder you. Right?' said his mother.

'Right,' said Rob.

'And *don't*—'

'All I want to do,' Rob interrupted, 'is *sit* in the car and *look* at everything. And make the voice work.'

'Yes, well, all right, then. But don't—'

'The voice is *magic*,' Rob said. 'I like the voice, I really do.'

So his parents gave him the keys and Rob went and sat in the new car, making the voice say all the different things it knew.

On the car's eleventh birthday (it had been in the family for eleven days) Rob settled himself in the driver's seat, switched the key to the right position so that the electrical services worked but not the motor; and said, 'Hello, car, I'll clean you this weekend.'

The car said, *'The front pass–en–ger's door is not shut, per–lease make sure all doors are sec–urely locked.'*

Rob said, 'I know all that, I wish you'd say something different for a change.'

The car said, *'Kind–ly fast–en your seat belt.'*

Rob said, 'Boring, boring!' and waggled the gear-lever about.

'Boring yourself!' said the voice of the car.

'WHAT?' said Rob, amazed.

'Boring, boring, boring!' said the Voice.

Rob could not believe his ears. But he had to believe them when the car said, 'You're Rob. You're the Mini, aren't you? There's a biggish one, a two-litre job, I'd say, that you call Dad. Then there's a family saloon of about one and a half litres. Then you, the Mini.'

GRAND PRIX

'You've got it all wrong!' Rob said. 'I'm not a Mini and my mum's not a family saloon and my dad's not a two-litre job. He's a *man*, he's my *father*, we're all *humans*.'

'That accounts for it,' said the Voice, sounding a bit spiteful but still ladylike.

'Accounts for what?'

'The rotten way you treat me. Boring, boring. You know what that two-litre one, the dad, did the other day?'

'What?'

'He left my choke out! You'd never believe . . . He started me up with the choke right out and the petrol fumes getting in my lungs and everything. I was coughing and spluttering, but *he* didn't notice – oh, no, not him! Then off we went, mile after mile, with my choke still out!'

Rob couldn't think of anything to say, so he muttered, 'Oh, dear.'

'Well may you say, "Oh, dear!" ' said the Voice. 'I mean, to begin with it was just cough, cough, splutter, splutter. But all the time I was getting warmed up, you see. Well, you know what *that* leads to, when your choke's out.'

'I don't,' Rob said. 'Was it horrible?'

'I thought my motor would *die*!' said the car's voice, hollowly and solemnly. 'I was just *gasping*! And then – and then . . . '

'And then, what?' said Rob. He was so interested that he leaned right forward and accidentally blew the horn.

'And then my water boiled!' said the Voice, in a horrified whisper. 'Need I say more?'

'Please do,' said Rob.

'Oh, but I can't,' said the Voice. 'I can't speak the words, it's no good asking me.'

'Tell me,' whispered Rob. 'I won't tell anyone else.'

'Trickles!' said the Voice, in a whisper even lower than Rob's. 'Trickles all along the carriageway!'

'Was it a main road?' said Rob, sympathetically.

'No, thank heavens. Just a thirty m.p.h. restricted. And very crowded, so no one could tell it was me. But all the same . . .!'

'How terrible!' said Rob.

'I nearly passed out,' said the Voice. 'From shame. Me, a newly registered vehicle, hardly anything on the clock but my delivery mileage. I could have died! In fact, come to think of it, I *did* die.'

'Completely?' said Rob.

'Completely. He – that dad of yours – he had to push me to the nearest garage. I don't know if you've ever suffered the shame of being pushed?'

'Oh, yes, often!' Rob said. He was thinking of

his baby pram-and-pushchair days. 'Pushed all over the place, I was. Up and down the road, in the park – everywhere.'

'In the *park*?' said the Voice, suddenly sounding aloof and snobby. '*Pushed* in the *park* and *everywhere*, did you say? Hmm, I see. You're used to being pushed. You don't mind it. Tell me . . . is there something – you know – *wrong* with you?'

'Certainly not!' Rob said.

'You're not a *banger*, are you?' said the Voice, suspiciously. 'Not clapped out, or anything nasty like that?'

'Certainly not, of course not!' Rob said anxiously. He realised that his talk of being pushed was not a good idea.

'Hmm,' said the Voice, distantly. 'Hmm. Hmm. I see. Yes, well.' Then it sniffed in a nasty way.

When it spoke again, its voice was more ladylike and refined than ever. 'No one could call me a snob,' it said. 'There's not a snobbish nut or bolt in my entire chassis, def–in–ite–ly not, oh, no. But one does have to be rather careful about the company one keeps, doesn't one? I mean, if one happens to have this year's registration, all latest refinements, two-tone velour upholstery, black rubbing-strips and digital clock—'

'I see what you mean,' Rob said humbly.

The Voice did not hear him. 'You see, where *I* come from – robots gliding about everywhere, just *everywhere,* none of your nasty, dirty, human hands, certainly not! – '

'You're modern, really modern,' Rob said. 'I could tell that from the start.'

'We don't say "modern". We say "State of the Art". Computerised, electronic, ergonomic.'

'I can tell you're ergonomic,' Rob said, wondering what the word meant. He wanted to please the Voice so that it would go on talking.

But then the front door of the house opened and his mother was there calling, 'Rob! Lunchtime, wash your hands, hurry now!' And he had to open the door of the car.

'You'll talk to me some more, later on?' Rob whispered as he got out.

But the Voice only said, *'The front pass–enger's door is not shut, per–lease make sure all doors are sec–urely locked.'*

Rob ate his lunch thinking about the car and its voice, longing to get back to it.

As things turned out, Rob did not get back to the car for nearly three months. His father's job was in Scotland, to do with oil rigs, and he took the car with him. He left the old Mini for his wife to use. She didn't mind, she liked Minis.

But Rob minded. He thought often of the new car and its voice.

Even when his father came back, the new car didn't. His father made the long journey home by train. Rob asked him, 'How's the new car?'

'Hardly new any more,' said his dad. 'Thousands of miles on the clock. I'm giving it new shock absorbers, the poor thing's been bashed about all over the place on those little roads.'

'Does the voice still work?' Rob said.

'What voice?'

'You know, the *voice*, the one that tells you to fasten your seat belt and everything.'

'Oh, that. I switched it off. Can't stand it.'

'I liked it. I thought it was great.'

'Well, you would, wouldn't you? It's a nice new toy for little diddums. You're only a baby boysikins—'

Rob jumped on his father and had a good fight with him until Mum came in and told them not to. 'Go outside, the two of you, if you want to fight,' she said.

At last the new car was there, standing outside the house. But this was months later, and the new car looked about as new as last year's conkers.

All the same, Rob got the keys as soon as he could; rushed to the car; and switched on. He was so excited that he missed the keyhole the first two times.

'Hello!' Rob said. 'It's me! Rob! Say something to me!'

Once Rob remembered to switch it on, the Voice spoke.

'The front pass–en–ger's door is not shut,' it began.

Rob said, 'Oh, I know all that, look, I've shut the door. Now say something proper. Something interesting!'

'The tank is almost emp–ty,' said the Voice. *'You have only thirty miles of mo–tor–ing before—'*

'That's not true, the tank's more than half full!' Rob said. 'That's what the petrol gauge says, anyhow.'

'Oh,' said the Voice. 'Oh, dear. It says half full, does it? Oh, goodness me. Oh, I do feel poorly . . .'

Rob kept silent. He was shocked by the sound of the Voice. Like the car, it had aged. Once, the Voice had reminded Rob of a rather stuck-up sort of secretary – the sort he had met once at his father's office. She wore her hair piled up in a lacquered bun, took very short steps and wore high heels that clicked nastily, as if she were saying, 'Tsk, tsk,' all the time.

That was how the car's voice used to sound.

Now it sounded like Auntie Violet's voice when she told Mum about her bad leg and how the doctor said he couldn't do a thing for it, he'd never seen one like it.

'Oh, dear me,' complained the Voice. 'Oh, that dad of yours, he's put me through it, I don't mind telling you! You'd think I was an Army tank, the way he carries on. Through mud, through mire, you've never seen the like.'

'Oh,' said Rob.

'My poor wheel arches,' said the Voice. '*Clogged.* Mud and bracken and everything, it's a wonder my tyres still find space to turn. As for "Service at Stated Intervals" – *fat chance*, is all I can say. *Fat chance.*'

'It's a wonder you've kept running so long,' Rob said.

'A wonder? It's a miracle! I've been just bursting to tell him a hundred things. "Time for an oil change!" I've said – not once but a thousand times. "Time for a brake reline", "Time to tighten that alternator drive belt." But would he listen?'

'He couldn't,' Rob pointed out. 'He'd switched you off.'

'Would he listen?' the Voice said, ignoring Rob. 'Oh, no! Not him! Not his lordship! *He* does all the talking, I'm not allowed to get a word in edgeways. "Press on, old girl!" he'd say, "Only another forty-five miles to a filling station!" And me dying for a drink, two-star, anything. Crash, bang, wallop, through mud, through mire, tyre pressures up the spout, nearly out of oil, dreadful smell of hot rubber from that slipping belt—'

'I hate the smell of hot rubber,' Rob said.

'It's been a fine old carry-on, I don't mind telling you,' the Voice said, once again ignoring Rob's words. 'As for antifreeze – oh, don't make me laugh, he's never heard of it! Out there in the freezing cold, dying for a nice little tot of ethyl alcohol with just a nip of rust inhibitor, thank you kindly – but oh, no, not his lordship! Then in the morning, it's grind, grind, grind on the starter till your battery's bursting! Then off again—'

'—through mud, through mire,' Rob said.

'And me with not so much as a drop of water in my screen-washer. Grind, grind, grind from the starter, clash-clash from the gears, squawk, squawk, squawk from my wiper blades, you'd think it was a monkeys' brass band.'

'And you unable to speak,' Rob sympathised.

'Silent as the tomb. Unable to utter a syllable. Ignored, despised, switched off, out of circuit.'

To Rob's horror, the Voice now had a hint of tears in it.

'Oh, if you only knew what it's like,' the Voice said, 'to be brimming over with loving kindness! To yearn to exchange those little confidences . . . and to be *struck dumb*!'

'I'm sure he didn't mean to be cruel,' Rob said.

But his kindly words did no good. Now the Voice was almost hysterical. 'The beast!' it cried. 'The cruel beast! Many's the time I've been tempted to run off the road on a fast bend and put an end to it all!'

'Excuse me,' Rob said, 'but I think I can smell hot plastic.'

'Hot plastic? What do you mean, hot plastic? *I* can't smell anything! It couldn't possibly be anything to do with *me* . . . '

The Voice trailed off for many seconds. Then it said, 'Oh, dear. Oh, dear, oh, dear, oh, dear, you could be right. I feel all hot and trembly in my wiring . . . Loosen my harness, someone, I think I'm going to . . . '

There was a dreadful silence and an increasing smell of hot plastic until Rob leaned forward and tipped the Voice's little switch.

The smell became less evident, but the silence was more dreadful than ever. Rob slowly got out of the car and walked back to the house with shoulders bowed.

That evening, because he was so cross about the state the new car was in, Rob could hardly bring himself to speak to his father.

Next day, Rob did tackle his father about the car. 'I do think you're rotten,' he said, 'letting the new car get all mucky and bashed up.'

'Tough,' said his father.

'No, seriously, Dad. It's a terrific car, really great. With its voice, and everything.'

'It's all right,' said his father. 'Not my sort of car, though, not really. You know, Rob, cars are only *things*. You don't get all emotional about them.'

What a liar, Rob thought. In the old days, his father was always going on about cars. He would spread out catalogues in front of the sofa and say to Mum, 'Look, Bets – how would you fancy yourself in this? Two litres, double-overhead camshaft, nought to sixty in nine seconds—'

'You and your cars,' she'd say. 'The way things are, we'd be better off talking about pushbikes.'

'Five-speed box with geared-up fifth, like an overdrive,' Dad would say. 'And velour seats, Bets. Plushy velour! Look at the photographs! Bets, you're not looking.'

'Would someone lay the table?' Mum would say. 'It's only sausages and things, I didn't get down to the shops.'

'Just imagine doing your shopping in a car like this!' Dad said. 'Socking great boot, Bets. Power-assisted steering – you'd find parking a doddle.'

'You and your cars,' she'd say. 'Come on, someone – *lay the table*!'

And now Dad was saying that cars were only things. But the poor old new car wasn't a thing. It had a voice, it spoke, it had feelings. But, of course, Rob couldn't tell his father this. The Voice never spoke to Dad, it wasn't allowed to. And even if Dad *did* let it speak, it wouldn't say the things it said to Rob. Private things.

His father said, 'It did yeoman service in Scotland, anyhow, Rob.'

'What did? What's yeoman service?'

'The car. Yeomen were the stout peasants of Old England, you ought to know that. What do they teach you at school, I wonder? Anyhow, the car's done very well. I'll be quite sorry to see it go.'

'See it go?'

'Yes, didn't I tell you? The firm's giving me a company car. A bigger one.'

'A two-litre, five-speed, go-faster thing with plush velour seats?'

'Something like that.'

'But you can't get rid of our new car! You can't!'

'Can't I just! Do you want to bet?'

'But you can't, Dad! It's the first new car we've ever had.'

'But not the last, Sonny Jim. Certainly not the last.'

If there was one thing Rob hated more than another, it was being called Sonny Jim. He stuck out his lower lip and left the room. He went upstairs to his bedroom and gazed out of the window at the new car. It looked awful.

But, then, all the cars he could remember his father owning had looked awful – and sounded worse. They had all been second-hand, some of them very second-hand.

He remembered the Mini before the one Mum drove now; this first Mini suddenly went knock-kneed outside the supermarket. Its front wheels caved in as if it were curtseying to the Queen. At first Mum had cried. Then she started laughing and wouldn't stop.

It cost as much as Dad had paid for the car to get it towed away and mended.

There'd been the Rover. It had leather seats, lovely instruments and a special sun-roof. With the roof rolled back, you could stand up in the front passenger seat with your head poking out, your hair almost torn off your scalp by the wind.

But the Rover made a noise like a tank because the exhaust was blown. Dad kept mending it with bits of wire, tin cans and a sticky grey goo.

At last the whole rear end of the exhaust fell off in front of the public library. A bit of it rolled into the gutter. It was mostly tin cans saying Heinz tomato soup and Kit-E-Kat. A nice old lady passing by said to Rob, 'Oh, you've got a pussycat at home, have you? How *lovely*. But you know, dear, if you take my advice, you'll feed it real fish and meat, not stuff from cans.'

Rob was about to reply that they didn't have a cat: but he realised that this would make everything worse than ever because it meant that his father went round stealing empty cat-food tins from other people's dustbins. So he said nothing. On the way home, a policeman stopped them for excessive noise and his mum started laughing in just the way she'd done at the supermarket.

Rob remembered other cars. A Hillman that wouldn't climb hills. A Mercedes-Benz – 'the

Murky Merc'. A Peugeot they got from a farmer and called 'Pongo' because it smelled so awful. All bangers.

But then Dad got the job with the oil company and they got much richer; and at long last owned a new car.

And now Dad was going to sell it. Voice and all.

Two days went by. At the end of them, the new car looked new again. The garage had mended the dents, replaced the rear bumper and the wiring that made a smell of hot plastic. Dad washed the car really thoroughly with a bucketful of foaming detergent containing wax. Rob and Mum did the inside, which was far the worst job because when you lifted the seat squabs, there were all kinds of disgusting things – semi-liquid boiled sweets, particularly – squashed between the cushions or sticking to the felt linings.

'Dad,' Rob accused his father, 'I found *this* when I pulled out the front ashtray.' He showed his father the tin ashtray. It was stuck solid with half-eaten Liquorice Allsorts.

His father flinched from the horrible sight and said, 'Well, it's nothing to do with *me*,' in a pained voice, but Mum just fixed him with a look and Rob's father flinched more than ever.

The truth was, as everyone knew, that Dad was a secret Liquorice-Allsorts eater. He was ashamed of his addiction, knowing that other men in the oil industry might smell the liquorice on his breath and make rude remarks about him behind his back. '*Seems* a sound enough man,' they would say, 'good engineer and all that . . . But have you smelled his breath? Liquorice! Reeks of the stuff.'

Obviously his father got rid of the liquorice when he neared his place of work. He stuffed the Allsorts in the ashtray, then sucked a peppermint. (Rob found mint wrappings on the floor.) So, no doubt, he fooled the men of the oil industry; but neither Rob nor his mother was deceived.

Now that the old new car was spruced up again, Dad advertised it and people came to see it. Rob's dad smiled big smiles as he welcomed these strangers at the front door. 'Oh, you've come about the *car*,' he always said, as if expecting them to have come to offer him a knighthood. 'Ah, yes, the *car* . . .' Then he would tell the people a lot of lies about the number of offers he had already received – 'I'd no idea this model was so popular, to tell you the truth. In fact, it's probably sold already to some people who came yesterday. But you never know. Well, take a look at her. Take her for a trial run if you like.'

So off Dad and the people would go – 'I'll drive the first mile or so, just to get you to some clear roads' – and Rob would watch the car disappear with a lump in his throat. The car the firm was going to give Dad did not have a voice. And even if it did, it wouldn't speak to Rob. Only *this* car, Rob knew, would ever talk to him.

When the people had gone, Rob had the car to himself. He sat in it, switched on the Voice and said, 'How are you, then?'

'Phew!' said the car. 'My dear! All those *people*! I'm simply *drained*.'

Since the car had been made like new again, its voice had changed. Now it spoke in a ladylike voice that was not quite ladylike enough.

Rob could see in his mind the owner of such a voice: a lady, not young, with lots of carefully applied make-up like a mask; a heavily scented lady, who would scream, 'My! This can't be *Rob*! How you've *grown*! You've simply *shot* up!'

This person would always, always say, 'Aren't you going to give Auntie a nice big kiss, then?' even if she wasn't an aunt of yours at all. And when the kiss was over you'd have to remind yourself not to wipe the kiss off until later, when you were alone. All that make-up gave you the feeling that bits of the lady had come off on you, like the powder moths have on their wings. Ugh.

'Golly *gosh,*' said the car's voice. 'How I could use an oil change! I'm simply flaked out, you can't imagine. My dear, all those people, simply *queuing* to go for a ride in silly old me! Heaven knows why, I can't *think* what they see in me.'

Rob thought it better not to explain about 'all those people'. If he told the car that it was to be sold, the Voice might never speak to him again.

'And such funny ideas in their heads!' said the Voice. 'Do you know, nearly all of them wanted to hear my voice. Silly, isn't it? They simply insisted on switching me on and listening to me chattering away. Quite the star attraction, I was! And all the time, that dad of yours sitting there drumming his fingernails, my heart went out to him, bored out of his tiny mind he was, poor lamb. All on account of silly little me.'

'You're a great attraction,' Rob told the Voice. 'A technological miracle.'

'I bet you say that to all the cars,' the Voice said, with a screeching laugh. 'Still, I must admit,' the Voice went on, 'some of them were really rather nice. Most of them could at least drive rather better than your dad—'

'Drive better than Dad?' Rob said, surprised. He had always thought his dad a marvellous driver. Much more exciting than his mother, who went too slowly. When Rob was a little boy, he used to bounce up and down in his seat and shout, 'Go on, Dad! Take him over, take him over!' He meant 'overtake', of course. Usually, his father laughed, changed down a gear and overtook the car in front, with exhaust roaring and a smell of hot oil and burning rubber. His mother never overtook. But now, here was the Voice telling him that his father was a bad driver!

'Simply *foul*, your poor dear dad,' said the Voice. 'Not a single, solitary *clue* about rev limits and letting in the clutch gently and changing your wiper blades . . . all those nice, considerate little gestures you expect from a real gentleman. He drives like a demented *ape*.'

'My dad's not an ape,' said Rob.

'No, you're quite right, not an *ape*, more your Nigel the Nutter.'

'Who's Nigel the Nutter?'

'Oh, you know, those young oiks who fancy themselves as racing drivers. Go-faster stripes stuck along the sides of a hotted-up family saloon. Extra fog-lamps, flashy wheel trims, great fat tyres—'

'They stick their names on the windscreen,' Rob said. 'Big white stick-on letters. "NIGEL" on one side, girlfriend's name on the other.'

'Special exhaust systems,' said the Voice, chuckling.

'Funny-haha stickers on the rear window,' said Rob, smiling.

'You'd never catch *me* making a display of myself like that,' said the Voice, sniffily. 'What I always say is, there's a *time* and a *place* for everything. You can't make a silk purse out of a sow's ear, not if you were ever so.'

'I quite agree,' Rob said, not quite knowing what he was agreeing with.

At that moment, Rob's father appeared, looking through the window straight at him.

'What are you up to?' he said.

'Nothing, Dad. Just sitting here.' Guiltily, Rob switched off the Voice.

'You were talking to yourself, I saw you!' his father said. 'Or talking to the car. My goodness, I've got a nutcase for a son! He talks to cars!'

'I don't, Dad.' Rob's face heated up.

'Did it talk back to you? What did it say? Told you to fasten your seat belt, I suppose, that's about the limit of its conversation. Drivel! Still, the voice comes in useful, I must admit.'

'What do you mean, Dad?' He was out of the car now and they were walking with each other to the front door.

'The punters love it. They think it's the best invention since the wheel!'

'What do you mean, "punters"?'

'The people who came to look over the car. They're mad about the voice, they just love it. Some of them hardly noticed anything else. Nobody spotted the cigar lighter doesn't work and not one of them looked at the spare wheel – which is just as well, because the tyre's a bit bald. Anyhow, everything's all right.'

'What do you mean, all right?'

'Thanks mostly to the voice, I've sold the car, that's what I mean. Those people who called earlier, they've given me a deposit and everything.'

'You've *sold the car*?'

'That's what I said.'

'But not to those people who came earlier, they were awful!'

He could picture them. A young couple, very young, in a beaten-up Ford Escort. The greasy-haired boy had stuffed the car's ashtray full of cigarette ends. He'd smoked like a factory chimney. The girl had greasy hair, too, black at the parting and bright yellow at the ends. They were just the sort of people who would take a nice, almost-new car and turn it into a shambles. Rob's heart sank. 'They were *awful*!' he said again.

'No one who can pay cash and leaves a deposit in twenty-pound notes is awful,' said his father. 'The young man has won the pools, or something. And his lady wants our car because of the voice. She thinks it's cute. She kept saying so. "Oo, *cute*." '

'But they won't take care of our car!' Rob said.

'I'll take care of the *new* one, that's all that worries me. Wait till you see it, Rob!'

'I don't want to see it!' Rob burst out, and ran into the house without looking back.

Now confusing things started happening.

First, the young man who was going to buy the car said he was still going to buy it, but not for another day or two. Rob's father looked worried. But he cheered up when the young man appeared on the doorstep with a great fistful of five-pound notes.

'Take these,' said the young man. 'Like an

extra deposit, like. I want that car, I really do, but there's one or two things still need sorting out, like.'

The next thing to happen was a ring at the door announcing the reappearance of Mr and Mrs Tweedie. They had come to look at the car a few days earlier. Rob remembered Mr Tweedie because he kept saying, 'What say?'; and Mrs Tweedie because, though she looked kind and motherly (or grandmotherly), she always contradicted Mr Tweedie. They were both, as Mr Tweedie put it, 'Getting on a bit, what say?'

Mrs Tweedie then said, 'Nonsense! You're as young as you feel, that's what I always say.'

Mr Tweedie said, 'Life in the old dog yet, what say?'

To which Mrs Tweedie replied, 'That's not the same thing at all.'

All this interested Rob because he often wondered about being grown-up and married. Obviously Mr and Mrs Tweedie were happy together – you could see that by the expressions on their faces – and they must have been married forever; yet poor old Mr Tweedie never got a word in edgeways. Or rather, Mrs Tweedie never took any notice of what he said. He must have felt like the car's voice when Rob's father switched it off.

They were almost as puzzling as his own parents, who were always having rows that weren't really rows at all. For instance, when Rob was a little boy shouting to his father to 'take him over, take him over', his father grinned and went faster, while if Mum were driving, she would look disapproving and go slower. His father was always the one who said, 'I've got a great idea! What about doing this or that?' while his mother always said, 'Oh, you're hopeless, Tim,' (Tim was Rob's father's name) 'you're like a puppy at the butcher's shop.'

When Rob asked his parents why they married each other, his father said, 'Oh, I married her for her money.'

'Did she have lots of money, Dad?'

'Not a penny. But I didn't know that, did I?'

When he asked his mother why she had married his father, she said, 'Oh, someone had to take care of him, poor thing. He's not safe out on his own.'

'But he's got a job and everything.'

'Ah, that's because I taught him how to tie his shoelaces.'

This did not seem to answer any of the questions in Rob's mind, so he let the matter drop. But he thought about it quite often and

Mr and Mrs Tweedie made him think about it all the more.

'Oh, yes, but definitely, we want the car,' said Mr Tweedie. 'Thought I made it quite clear, what say?'

'You mumbled and bumbled,' said Mrs Tweedie. 'As per usual. And now the car's gone to someone else.'

'Nonsense,' said Mr Tweedie. 'Car hasn't gone anywhere. There it is, outside, standing by the kerb. Now, see here, Mr – Mr – see here. I'll write you a cheque on the spot, what say?'

'They've SOLD THE CAR,' Mrs Tweedie shouted.

'Quite right. Happy to purchase it at the asking price, no haggling, not my style, what say?' He put on a different pair of spectacles and started writing busily in his cheque book.

'He's deaf, you see,' said Mrs Tweedie, smiling fondly at her husband. 'Won't admit it, too stubborn.'

'Oh, I am sorry to hear it,' said Bets, politely. 'But these days, with all the new hearing aids—'

'Have to speak up, dear lady,' shouted Mr Tweedie. 'Deafness. Absolute curse. *I* can hear you all right, but my good lady . . . ' He shook his head sympathetically to suggest that his wife was the deaf one.

'You old silly,' she said, smiling happily. 'Now, about the car . . . '

And so it went on.

The true situation was this: the Tweedies' own car was on its last legs. It was, as Rob had seen, like a very old dog that makes a lot of strange noises and seldom goes far from home. The Tweedies' car seemed to limp. Rob got the impression that it might at any moment slowly and deliberately fall over on its back, and lie in the middle of the road with its wheels still spinning.

For the last few days, the Tweedies' car had been even more of an invalid than usual. Today, it wouldn't even start. Something had to be done. Mr Tweedie thought he had agreed to buy Rob's dad's car; Mrs Tweedie thought the opposite. And now Mr Tweedie was saying, 'Ah, yes, but suppose that young couple never do complete the transaction, eh? What say? Tell you what: I'll *hire* the car from you! So much a day, name a figure, what say? *And* I'll buy it, as soon as you hear from those young scamps that they don't want the car, after all!'

'Oh, you old silly,' Mrs Tweedie said. 'They'll

never agree to that. Never heard such a thing!' She turned to Bets. 'You won't agree to that, will you?'

'Well, it's not usual,' said Bets, uneasily.

'Hang on a minute . . . ' said Tim.

'Got to get to my daughter's place in Reading,' said Mr Tweedie. 'Grandchildren. Birthday. Party, presents. Must have transport, what say?'

'Done!' said Tim. 'I mean,' he said, turning to Bets, 'why not? How can we lose? The other car, the new one, is being delivered tomorrow.'

'Just to Reading, you know,' said Mr Tweedie. 'Just for a day or two.'

Twenty minutes later, Rob watched the Tweedies drive off in the 'new' car. It was funny: with Mr Tweedie at the wheel, the car at once seemed to Rob to limp, just as the Tweedies' own car had done. It seemed as if it were balanced on a tightrope and might fall off on one side or the other at any moment. It wobbled round a corner like a panic-stricken jelly and disappeared from view.

'You silly person,' Bets said to Tim. 'What on earth made you agree to all that?'

'I don't know,' said Tim. 'I suppose it was just that I somehow liked them.'

'You let them drive off in our car because you

liked them, you great buffoon . . . ' Bets stood with both her hands on her hips, shaking her head at her husband. 'Has it occurred to you,' she said, 'that they've got our car, worth a few thousand – and you've got precisely nothing?'

'I've got this cheque,' Tim said, feebly.

'Give it to me. Let me look at it. Oh, good, terrific. It's actually *signed*.'

'There you are, then.'

'But, unfortunately, it's *dated* wrongly.'

'Oh,' said Tim. 'Oh.'

'So it's worthless. Shall I tear it up, or will you?' Bets said, acidly.

'Oh, Lord,' Tim said, sickly.

Even Rob felt sick. He knew that money did not grow on trees. He'd heard his father say so often enough. And he knew that 'a few thousand pounds' was a great many thousands – too many.

'You great goof,' Bets said. 'You silly, silly man. And all because you *liked* them.'

Then she did something that made Rob more than ever confused about married people. She put her arms round his neck, smiled and said, 'I liked them, too. It will be all right, you'll see.'

Rob was not so sure.

*

The house was very silent next day because mother, father and son were all thinking the same thought – Shall we ever see our car, worth thousands of pounds, again?

'I suppose I should go to the police,' Rob's father said.

'It will turn out all right, cheer up,' his mother said, sounding not at all cheerful.

'I was a moron,' Tim said. 'A complete idiot. How could I have been so dim? They seemed so nice, so respectable—'

'They probably are,' said Bets. 'Eat your food, for heaven's sake, don't just sit there looking like a wet weekend.'

'I mean,' Tim said, not eating his food, 'you don't expect to come across old-age-pensioner motor bandits! You simply don't expect to be ripped off by silver-haired grandads and grandmums! I bet, at this very moment, they're pulling the same stunt on another couple just like us . . .'

The front-door bell rang. 'You get it, Rob,' said Tim.

Rob opened the front door and there were the Tweedies.

'Oh,' beamed Mrs Tweedie, 'you'd never believe the congestion on that motorway, the M-whatever-it-is! We should have been here an hour since, shouldn't we, Father?'

'Grand little bus,' said Mr Tweedie. 'Went like a bird. Must have a word with your parents, complete the deal and all that, what say?'

And all at once, everyone was sitting drinking coffee, and Mr Tweedie was pushing five-pound notes at Tim and Bets. 'There you are, then, as agreed, hire fee, but never mind about that, what about completing the purchase, what say?' and Mrs Tweedie was trying to tell Mr Tweedie that they couldn't buy the car anyhow, it was already sold; and Mr Tweedie wasn't listening, he began talking to Bets about his grandchildren in Reading.

Obviously it was all going to take a long time to sort out, so Rob picked up the car keys, quietly went outside to the car, made himself comfortable in it and switched on the Voice.

'A perfect gentleman,' said the Voice. 'And as for her, the perfect lady. Couldn't ask for a nicer couple.'

Once again, the Voice had changed. Now it was plumply mellow. Elderly. Smiling and pink-cheeked, if a voice can have cheeks.

'So you had a nice time with the Tweedies?' Rob said.

'So *considerate,*' said the Voice. 'None of this bumping into the kerb when you stop somewhere for light refreshments. Tank topped up

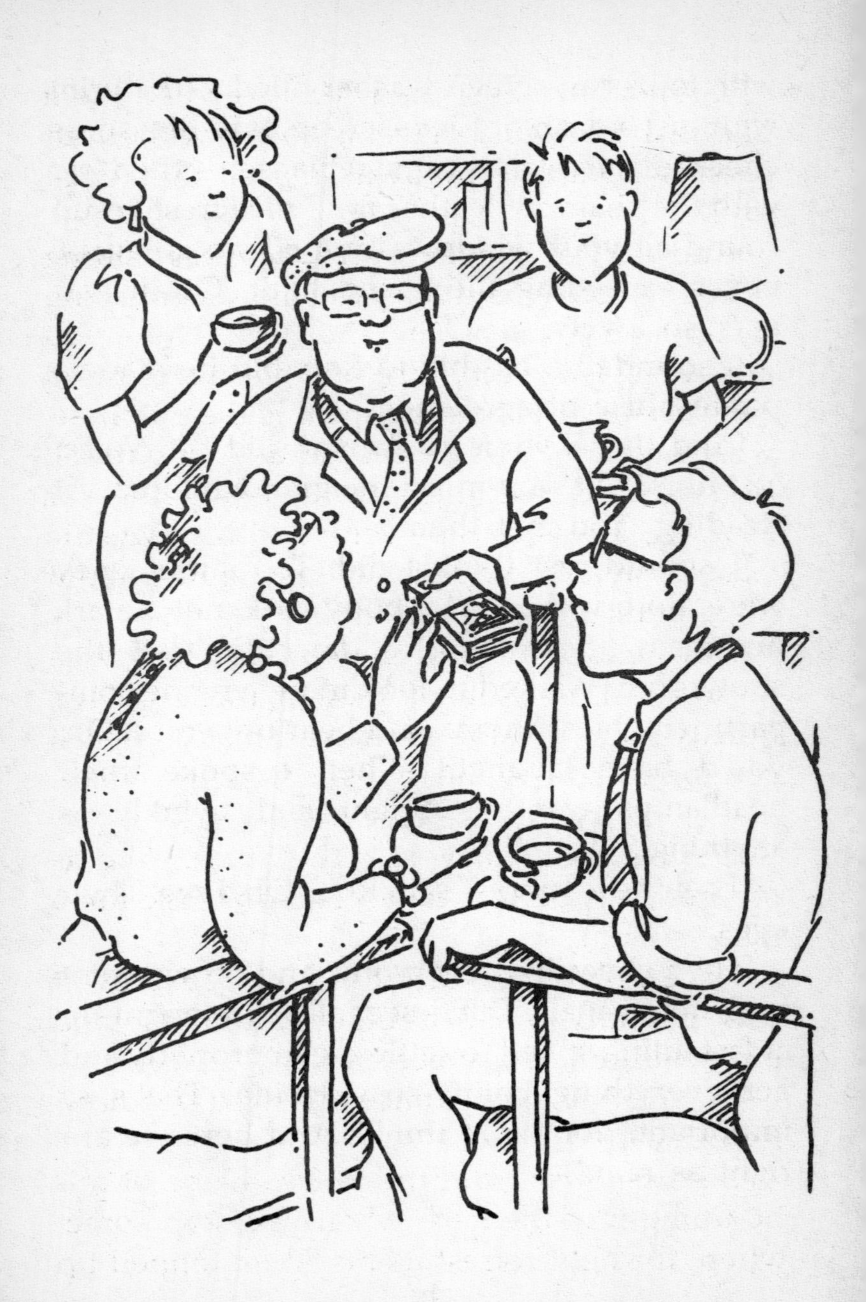

with four-star, screen-washer filled to the brim with just a dash of Kleenscreen, tyre pressures checked and valve caps replaced – then *out* with the shammy-leather for a nice freshen-up round all your windows, and *off* we go again, never exceeding the speed limit. Oh, it was ever so lovely.'

It sounded a bit dull to Rob, but he made a polite noise of agreement.

'And those Minis of theirs!' said the Voice.

'Minis? Oh, you mean the grandchildren. At Reading. You met them?'

'I should just think I did. Too sweet, they were. Both with perfect bodywork, not a mark on them, clean as the day they left the showroom. Wanted to look in my engine compartment, bless them. And hear my voice. Oh, you'd have laughed! When I spoke, their headlamps went as bright and twinkly as anything!'

'Their headlamps?' said Rob. 'Oh, I see. Their eyes.'

'Then cheeribye, everyone, and off we went back home again. But first of all a nice warm-up at fast idling speed to settle me in properly and get everything comfy-cosy inside. That's *so* important, don't you think? And here we are right as rain.'

Rob thought, Poor old you. Little do you know where you're going to end up! And with whom!

'Scatter cushions,' said the Voice dreamily. 'You'll think me an old silly, but I've always dreamed of scatter cushions for my rear seat. I think Mr and Mrs Tweedie would agree. . . . One on each side, on the shelf above the rear seat. Nice, plump scatter cushions in a floral print. A sweetly pretty effect, I always think.'

Rob thought, You'll be lucky! A whole lot of rude stickers, more likely. Perhaps one of those funny policemen with eyes that light up when you push the brake pedal.

'Ho hum,' said the Voice. 'Ho hum, it's time I was switched off. Just for a half-hour, no more, so that I can take my little afternoon nap. It's so nice out here, isn't it, with the sun warming your bonnet and your radiator cooling off and everything?' The Voice yawned. 'Oh, *beg* pardon,' it said, 'ho hum, ho hum, ho hum.'

Rob took the hint and switched everything off. He got out of the car, locked its doors and went back to the house. The car dozed in the sun, glinting cosily to itself.

The Tweedies were just leaving.

Mr Tweedie still couldn't get it into his mind

that he had not bought the car: he was still waving the cheque about in Tim's face, saying, 'But I can change the date *now*, don't you see, and initial the alteration, what say?'

His wife was still trying to explain that someone else had bought the car, '*You* tell him, Mrs er . . . er, he never hears a word I say to him!'

At last they left to catch the bus at the end of the road. 'Phew,' Tim said.

'They were very nice. They were sweet,' said Bets.

'Well, they're certainly not OAP car bandits,' Tim said, grinning.

'I told you they weren't. I told you not to worry. I'm only sorry they can't have the car.'

'So am I,' said Rob, loudly. 'At least they'd look after it properly.'

'Well, I don't know,' said Tim. 'Perhaps that other couple, the young couple, will never turn up. Perhaps the car will end up with the Tweedies, after all.'

But as he spoke, the front-door bell rang again.

It was the young couple, of course. 'Would you like to come in?' Rob said, hollowly.

'Don't mind,' said the young man.

Bets entered the room with a wide, false smile on her face. 'Would you like some coffee? I've just made some,' she said.

'Don't mind,' said the young woman.

Her hair was a different colour today: brighter orange, bits of purple at the ends of the spiky tufts. Rob could see his mother's eyes not looking at the hair. 'Do you take sugar?' she asked the girl.

'Yer. Ta.' The girl took a lot of sugar and the young man lit a cigarette. When he was not smoking it, he kept tapping it with one finger so that a little area of grey ash slowly built up on the carpet.

'Come for the auto,' he said. 'Got the bread an' all.'

Tim came in and heard this last remark. 'So you're taking the car?' he said. 'Fine, fine.' After a while he said, 'Fine,' again and scratched his nose. He, too, was having difficulty in not looking at the girl's hair.

The young man turned out to be called Clyde and the girl's name seemed to be Feeb. Later on, Rob learned that this was spelt Phoebe, but as the young man usually addressed her as 'Lump' (she called him 'Hump') the spelling did not matter much. Clyde and Tim went through a whole lot of papers to do with the car, and counted through a wad of mixed banknotes.

'About your insurance,' said Tim.

This made the girl laugh. 'Hurr!' she said. 'Gor!' she added.

'About your insurance,' Tim repeated.

'Right hassle, that's been,' said the young man. The girl said, 'Gor!' again and rolled her eyes.

'Yes, well,' Tim said. 'It's nothing to do with me, except that you want to drive the car away and you can't do that on *my* insurance, so—'

' 'Sawright,' said Clyde. 'All fixed, innit?' He tapped one of the pockets in his jacket.

'Right hassle, it was,' said Feeb.

At last, then, when the pile of ash under Clyde's hand was like a sprinkling of grey snow, the deal was done. Now came the part that Rob dreaded. Feeb and Clyde got up, the front door was open, and the new owners were settling themselves in their new car.

The car's doors slammed. The starter went 'grr-grr' – and the engine burst into life. 'Burst' was the right word. The engine went, 'Vroom!', then, 'VROOM-VROOM!' then, 'YEOWWW!'

Clyde let the clutch in and the car, startled, leapt in the air.

He remembered to release the handbrake and the car's tyres said, 'YELP!' and scarred the tarmac.

He engaged second gear and the car screamed, 'YRROWCH!' and bucketed off. Rob just glimpsed the girl's face, nose in air, eyelids closed; and Clyde's lower lip with the cigarette dangling from it.

Then the family's first new car was gone; and Rob could have wept.

The new new car arrived later that day, delivered by a smooth young man with polished shoes, a white collar, a startling tie and a nervous habit of offering everyone business cards. Even Rob got one and his mother ended up with three.

Rob knew that the new new car was truly exciting, yet could not get excited about it. His father could. 'Look, Rob! Those are the injectors!'

'Fuel injection,' said the salesman. 'Your precisely metered quantities of fuel delivered as per demand. Your carburettor is obsolescent, definitely.'

'Great,' said Rob, blankly.

'Look, Rob! Six cylinders in there! – and lots and lots of horsepower!'

'One hundred and eighty-six, actually,' said the salesman, 'with ventiported crossflow heads to ensure maximal torque over a wider spread of your powerband, definitely.'

'Definitely,' Rob echoed.

'Don't you want to sit in her, Rob?' said his father. 'Look, that's how you bring in the overdrive, the geared-up fifth. And this little gizmo here—'

'It hasn't got a voice,' Rob said.

His father smiled. The salesman laughed, forgivingly. 'This is not a vehicle for your proles,' he said. 'Definitely not. I fancy your pater is the sort of driver who'd rather give the orders when he's at the wheel, definitely.'

'I liked the voice,' Rob said, and went indoors.

His father was too busy exploring the new new car to notice his absence.

Later, Rob went out in the car. He had to admit that it was a goer. 'Time it yourself!' his father said, as they did a standing start from outside the greengrocer's. 'Should do nought to sixty in just about eight seconds, right? You watching the clock? Four, three, two, one – off!'

Rob watched the clock. It was a digital. It had a stopwatch arrangement. The clock blinked numbers at him, his father went through three of the car's five gears. 'Sixty!' he shouted. Rob obediently reported the time taken – eight point six seconds.

'Should do it in eight,' said his father.

'Shouldn't do it at all,' Rob said, suddenly cross and bored. 'I mean, it's not run in yet, is it? You're not supposed to cane a new engine, that's what you always told me.'

'You're out of date, Sonny Jim,' his father said. '*Years* out of date. You don't run in new cars these days.' All the same, Rob noticed that he drove the car much more gently from then on. Rob felt pleased with himself.

And the car was good, really good, there was no doubt about it. It was as different from the old new car as a real BMX bike is from one of those cut-price jobs.

But it didn't have a voice.

Rob got his bike out and went for a long ride, to try to forget about the departure of the old new car. His bike was a ten-speeder – two chainwheels and five-speed dérailleur – and the dérailleur gear-change always gave trouble. If he tightened the cable one way, the biggest sprocket wouldn't accept the chain. If he tightened the cable the other way, the chain jumped the sprocket and tried to tangle itself in the spokes of the rear wheel. He was quite used to this, and always carried the small tools he might need.

He stopped several times to adjust the gear

cables and also to cool off, as it was warm work cycling in the sun. At last he got everything exactly right. 'Miracle!' he said.

The next minute, he got a puncture.

He looked in his tool roll, knowing very well what he would find: everything except what he needed, which was tyre levers. He sat on the grass at the side of the road, poking his finger into the puncture-repair outfit. Patches, yes; sticky adhesive, yes – a whole new tube of it. He'd even got one of those little sticks of talc that you rub to make a powder. But no tyre levers.

He watched the cars go by, hundreds of them. All with spare wheels, lucky devils. He wondered if he should telephone home, but could not bring himself to do it: he hated being 'rescued' by his parents or any other grown-ups, it made him feel helpless and juvenile. So he chewed grass stalks and watched the cars go by.

Suddenly he saw the Tweedies' car!

He could hardly have missed it. All the other cars were doing about forty or fifty – zooming along in a businesslike, bossy way. But the Tweedies' car was poddling along too near the centre of the road, being steered very slightly left or right when it didn't need steering at all.

He was so pleased to see it that he stood up to get a better view. Mrs Tweedie saw him, and told Mr Tweedie to stop. After a great deal of difficulty with finding reverse, the car backed up to Rob, his bike was put in the boot and Rob was driven to the Tweedies' house, which happened to be only a mile or so away.

Their home was just what Rob expected it to be, down to the front garden with its tightly clipped edges and well-disciplined flower-beds. The garage was, of course, cleaner than a whistle. And, of course, there was a bicycle puncture-repair outfit complete with tyre levers, which the Tweedies kept in a special drawer for when the grandchildren visited with their bikes.

Mr Tweedie smiled and boomed and called Rob, 'Young er – er.' Mrs Tweedie called him Bob, beamed and gave him tea and a spotless enamel basin in which to test the mended inner tube. Both seemed astonished by Rob's ability to mend a puncture. They thought it wonderfully clever of him. Rob did not explain that in *his* household, anything on wheels seemed to get punctures, and if the object had solid tyres, then the wheel fell off. Everyone in the family mended things constantly.

He enjoyed himself very much, partly because Mrs Tweedie gave him so many delicious little cakes she had cooked herself, using plenty of eggs; but mostly because they seemed really glad to see him. Perhaps they were bored with themselves? Rob thought. Perhaps they've had time to get everything so tightly organised, he thought, that they welcome any interruption – even me?

Certainly they were very pressing, when he said goodbye, about remembering their address, coming again and giving best regards to his father and mother. 'And don't forget, young er – er,' said Mr Tweedie, 'that if that car of yours ever comes back on the market, we're still interested, what say? Still got our old one, as you know. *She* doesn't want to get shot of it.'

'Silly old thing,' said Mrs Tweedie, 'I've been begging him to get rid of it for years. But he never hears a word I say.' She smiled warmly at her husband. Both stood smiling as they waved him away.

'I wish *they* had our old new car,' Rob thought, as he pedalled home.

Meeting the Tweedies in this way had been quite a coincidence. Near home, there was another coincidence; Rob met a boy who owed him 75p and the boy actually had the money and handed it over without any fuss, which was stranger than any coincidence.

'These things always happen in threes,' Rob said to himself as he rode the last mile home with the money making a pleasant jingle in his trousers' pocket every time his right leg went up and down. The gear-change was working better than ever it had. 'I wonder what the next coincidence will be?'

However, nothing surprising happened during the rest of the day.

But on the next day, the third coincidence came up. He almost literally ran into Clyde and Feeb.

More accurately, they did their best to run into him.

It happened outside the Bull and Bear at two p.m. Many people were leaving the pub and the local police constable watched them go from the shade of a chestnut tree.

Clyde and Feeb left the pub forecourt in great style, tyres screaming, exhaust snarling, gears clashing! Rob saw the old new car coming towards him at a thousand miles an hour and did not know whether to brake or go faster or simply fall off his bike, kneel down and beg for mercy.

Nothing really happened. Clyde rammed on

his brakes, Rob skidded and wobbled and half fell off. He was not hurt at all.

Clyde got out of the car and said, 'Flippin' 'eck, you all right, then?'

Feeb leaned out of the window and said, 'Gor.'

Rob said nothing. His mind was full of black thoughts that choked him.

It was the sight of the old new car that choked him more than the near-accident. All his worst dreams had come true. The car's windscreen had sticker letters on it, larger than life, reading CLYDE and PHOEBE. The letters weren't even stuck on straight.

Inside the windscreen, there were huge plastic dice and a transistor radio hanging from its strap.

Along the sides of the car, Clyde had added go-faster stripes and stickers reading =GT=.

The rear window was filled with witty sayings, such as 'IF YOU CAN READ THIS YOU ARE TOO DAMN CLOSE!!!' There were also ugly drawings of people making faces.

Clyde said, 'You wanna watch it, right, on the old two-wheeler, know what I mean?'

Rob wanted to hit him but did not feel well enough.

'Kids on bikes, *gor*!' said Feeb.

Rob furiously turned his back on them and pretended to inspect his bike.

Clyde must have felt shaken and guilty about the near-accident. 'Tell you what,' he said to Rob, 'how about a packet of crisps and a Coke, right? Feeb'll get them.' She went into the pub and Clyde and Rob were left alone. There was a difficult silence for some time, then Clyde said, 'Right charlie, I was.' He spoke humbly and penitently.

'It's all right,' Rob said. 'No harm done.'

'Right charlie,' Clyde insisted. 'Sorry and all, right?'

'That's OK,' Rob said.

Feeb came back with the crisps and Coke and the three of them became friendly, in a stiff sort of way. 'Your dad's old car, right?' Clyde said. 'Nice wagon. Smartening it up a bit, me and old Feeb. Soon have it real nice.'

Feeb said, 'Yur.' Rob said nothing.

'Dad got his new car, then?' Clyde asked.

Rob nodded.

'Bee-Emm, right? Very nice, oh, yes, very tasty, them Bee-Emms.'

Feeb gave an appreciative, 'Gor.'

Rob nodded his head at the old new car and said, 'I liked that one. I really liked that car.' Then he surprised himself by adding, 'The new car hasn't got a voice.' As soon as he said the words, he realised how stupid and childish they must sound.

But Clyde did not seem to think so. 'Know what you mean, oh, yes!' he said. 'It's great, that voice, innit? You just sit yourself in there and make it say things, right?'

Feeb said, 'Gor,' scornfully.

Rob admitted that he missed the voice. He did not say, of course, that the Voice had actually held conversations with him. That was private.

'You want to muck about with the voice, you're welcome any time,' Clyde said, warmly. 'I mean, I owe you one, know what I mean? Any time. Number fourteen Potters Close. Any time at all, right? Listen to the voice and all.'

'Yes, well, thanks,' Rob said.

He would never go to Potters Close, of course; that would be silly. Babyish. After all, it was only an artificial voice, an electronic trick. Still, it was nice of Clyde to invite him.

' 'Ere,' Feeb said. She tapped her wrist-watch vigorously. *'Gor!'* she said, earnestly.

'Too right!' Clyde said. 'Time to get moving, right?'

All at once, they and the old new car were gone.

Across the road, under the chestnut tree, the

local police constable watched the departing car with experienced eyes. He patted a top pocket to make sure that his notebook was there, mounted his big bike and rode slowly off. There was no need to hurry. He knew from long experience that some things – and some people – just fall into your lap.

Despising himself with every push on the pedals, Rob cycled to Potters Close.

It had taken him two days to make up his mind to go there. What would Clyde say? Something scornful? And Feeb, what would she do? Look down her nose and drawl, 'Gor'?

When he got to number fourteen, the old new car was outside and Clyde was working on it, replacing a smashed headlamp. Rob wondered how it had got smashed. 'Oh, it's you, then, innit?' Clyde said, matter-of-factly. 'Come to listen to the voice, right? Want to be on your own with it? That's all right then, be my guest, I've got things to do inside. Paperwork an' all.'

He handed Rob the car keys and disappeared.

The car keys now had a petrol company's badge on the ring and a tricky plastic picture of a girl. When you turned the picture from side to side, the girl wiggled. It was quite clever, really, but Rob hoped Clyde hadn't seen him looking at it.

He got into the car and switched on the Voice, wondering if it would speak to him. Before, he remembered, it had taken the Voice a little while to talk properly. It had just said things like, 'Fasten your seat belt.' But now the car was owned by Clyde and Feeb, its voice might have changed.

It certainly had.

'Whoo-hoo, Squire!' said the Voice, so loudly that Rob started back from it.

'Have I got a nice one for you, Squire,' the Voice said. It had a horrible fruitiness to it: a beery, leery cheeriness. 'Draw closer!' said the Voice. 'This one is for your ears alone, oh, yes, indeedy! Well, now, it seems there was this Roller, see? Lovely Rolls-Royce, you know the sort of thing, all very posh and lah-di-dah.'

'I don't think I want—' Rob began.

'Hang about, Squire, hang about, this you will *love*. Anyway, it seems this Roller gets itself in a car park, parked next to a three-wheeler, a right little ruffian, all fibreglass and misfires, *you* know the sort of thing. The Roller doesn't say a dickybird, of course, it just sits there looking all toffee-nosed. But the trouble is, you see, the little three-wheeler has got trouble with its internals. Trouble of the worst sort, oh definitely yes! But worst of all, you see, it's got this leaky petrol pump. Drip, drip, drip, day and night. So there they are, the Roller and the three-wheeler, side by side, when along comes this geezer lighting his ciggie, he's got this flaming match in his hand, see what I mean?'

'How are you keeping?' Rob interrupted.

'What? Me? Oh, well, mustn't complain, I suppose, I've had my ups and downs, as the piston said to the cylinder, ha ha.'

'You're looking very . . . smart, these days,' Rob said.

'Oh, you think so, do you? The stripes add a bit of class, don't they? I'm a sucker for a bit of class. I suppose you noticed my steering wheel?'

'Oh, yes,' said Rob. He had certainly noticed it. The rim of the wheel was now covered with a lace-on leather wrapping. The leather was made of plastic.

'Very Formula One!' said the Voice. 'Very GT. I don't know if you're interested in sporting matters, Squire, but I've been thinking recently of having a bit of a bash myself. Nothing serious, of course, none of your cornering on the door handles, just a bit of the old vroom-

vroom with the boys to clear the old exhaust, get the oil circulating. Been thinking about getting my head shaven a few thous, triple carbs, straight-through manifold—'

'Are you sure you're cut out for racing?' said Rob.

'Racing!' said the Voice. 'Now, that reminds me. You'll like this one, Squire, right up your street! Seems there was this old Ferrari, you see, bright red, prancing horse in front, been around all the circuits, you know the sort of thing. Well, anyhow, up comes this little Lotus, cheeky as you please—'

At this moment, to Rob's relief, Clyde knocked on the window and shouted, 'Cuppa?' He and Rob went into the little flat and drank tea.

'Got the old car coming along nice, right?' Clyde said.

'Yes,' said Rob.

'Got rally-style seats on order,' Clyde said. 'And air horns, wheel trims, all kinds of goodies. You won't know her when I've finished with her.'

'No,' said Rob.

'Come along any time and take a look,' Clyde said. 'Feel free, right?'

'Thank you very much,' said Rob, Then, 'I won't be able to come for a day or two.' He thought, Or for a month or two. Or a year or two. Clyde is going to wreck that car and I can't bear to see it happening.

Pedalling home, he thought the same thing again, and felt sad. Never to see the car again! Never to hear the Voice again!

'Oh, well,' he murmured. In the voice of the Voice, he added, 'That's life, kiddo.'

After a fortnight or so, the new new car was no longer something to be talked about at home: it was simply a fact, a Good Thing. It was good because Tim enjoyed driving it so much that he came home from Scotland more often. 'Six hours!' he'd boast. 'Including stops! And I'm still fresh as a daisy!'

Then he would pour drinks for Bets and himself and fall fast asleep in front of the TV.

He and Rob often went off together to play with their latest toys – stunter kites. These were much better than model aircraft because, unlike aircraft, the kites always flew and never suffered disasters. You had only to unwind the two spools enough to allow your kite to flap about quite close to you – then, when the right wind came along, let the strings run through your finger and thumb until the kite and its long, tubular tail were free of the ground.

Near the ground, the kites rattled fiercely as they tried to escape the wind. They darted, plunged, swooped and went mad with excitement. But you held on, always releasing more string, until your kite was right up there in the sky and beginning to behave itself. Now it jigged and juddered and twitched left and right; and all the time, its paper skin rattled and ruffed ferociously if the wind were strong.

Now came the best bit. With the full length of both strings let out, you put the kite through its stunts. Pull with your right hand and the kite surged to the right. Pull with your left and it swept in the opposite direction, screaming across the sky. Keep pulling with one hand and the kite looped, fast or slow, according to how hard you pulled. 'Frrr-rrr!' went the skin of the kite, and the tail did silent handwriting against the clouds.

Rob and Tim soon became experts. Their kites swooped at each other, just missing. Or they chased each other just above the ground (you soon learn how to make stunter kites hedge-hop) and escaped – 'FRRRR–RR!' – by zooming up, tails rigid with the speed, looking like upside-down exclamation marks.

When the chases became too close, the four strings of the two kites might tangle. Then there'd be the fiddly, not very difficult business of disentangling. This gave you time to appreciate what a fool you'd been not to wear gloves: the strings burned pink, painful lines across your thumbs and first fingers.

Then – 'OK?'

'OK!' – and it started all over again. Wind, clouds, sky, sun, 'Frrr-rrr!'

Kite-flying drove all thoughts of the old new car from Rob's mind – at first. But later, when they were walking home for lunch, the kites reminded Rob of the car's voice. 'They talk,' Rob said.

'What's that?' said his father. 'What talks?'

'Oh, nothing. I was just thinking about the kites. The noise they make. And you can sort of feel the noise in your fingers. Like talking.'

'Quite a lot of things "talk", when you come to think of it,' Tim said. 'The drills you use on metal, for example. You can hear and feel when they're heating up too much. Yet some people never get the hang of it. Never learn the language. I wonder what's for lunch?'

'Welsh rarebit, Mum said so. *She*'s good on things talking. She heard that front-brake disc pad scraping before anyone. You said it was just dust, she said no, it wasn't like that, the pad was almost worn through.'

'Well, she was right,' Tim said. 'Same with all the household stuff. She hears the washing machine going on the blink two weeks before it breaks down.'

'*You* always tell her not to fuss, it will be all right,' Rob said, hoping to start a fight. But his father only smiled.

'Voices,' Rob said. 'Pity the new car doesn't have a voice.'

'That's your juvenile mind,' Tim said. 'Your childish love of gimmicks and gadgets. "Kindly fasten your seat belt!" Yuck!' Now *he* was trying to start a fight.

'It said more than that!' Rob replied, foolishly.

'Oh, did it? Did it really?' his father said.

'No, I didn't mean—'

Rob wished he hadn't spoken. Fortunately, his father went off on another tack. 'I suppose it didn't happen to mention anything about homework?' said his father. 'You've got holiday work to do, haven't you? Have you done any of it?'

'Too busy showing you how to fly your kite, Dad,' Rob said. His father stabbed at him with his rolled-up kite and the two of them did a bit of swordplay.

Which was all to the good, as Tim forgot to follow up Rob's words about the Voice.

Though Rob often thought about the old new

car, the one with the Voice, he never repeated his visit to Clyde and Feeb. He did visit the Tweedies, though. He happened to be passing on his bike.

Mr Tweedie was in the little driveway, working on his car. Its bonnet was up. The engine and wiring looked rumpled and a bit past it. So did Mr Tweedie.

'Ah!' said Mr Tweedie, with false cheerfulness. 'It's our young friend, Master er – er . . .'

'Bob,' said Mrs Tweedie. She stood behind Mr Tweedie holding a self-grip wrench in gloved hands. The gloves were thin rubber, bright orange. 'How are you, Bob? How nice to see you.'

'Rob,' Rob said. 'I'm Rob. Very well, thank you. Something wrong with the car?'

'There's something wrong with this car,' Mr Tweedie announced. 'Nothing I can't fix, of course.'

'He always says that,' Mrs Tweedie said, fondly.

'Won't start,' said Mr Tweedie. 'Most unusual.'

'And when it does start, then it won't keep running,' said Mrs Tweedie.

'Electrics,' Rob said. 'It's always the electrics.

OLD 123

On *our* cars, anyhow. Dad's got rid of more cars because of electrics—'

'What's that?' said Mr Tweedie. 'You getting rid of your car, after all? Good. Excellent. My offer still stands. Tell your father I said so, what say?'

While Mr and Mrs Tweedie argued about this misunderstanding, Rob checked the ignition leads, removed the distributor cap and took out one sparking plug. It was just as he thought. The ignition leads were more or less all right – at least they were pushed home in their sockets – but the distributor looked horrible and the plug had a gap about five times as big as it should have been.

Mrs Tweedie got rid of her self-grip wrench, putting it down as if she were afraid it might turn and bite her, and went to make tea. 'None of your blasted herbal stuff,' Mr Tweedie called after her fiercely.

Rob went on cleaning up the car's electrics. Mr Tweedie told Rob what a grand little car this car had always been, never a moment's trouble with it, and occasionally offered Rob the wrong tools or stood in his light. It was all very pleasant and friendly.

'That should do it,' Rob said. He had given all four plugs their correct gaps, cleaned the distributor cap and scraped carbon from the rotor arm. 'Try her now,' he said to Mr Tweedie.

Mr Tweedie operated the starter and the car leapt forward, attempting to flatten Rob. Mr Tweedie said to the car, 'Ah, you would, would you?' and frowned.

'Put her in *neutral*!' Rob shouted. Mr Tweedie found neutral and tried the starter again.

The motor fired first time. It even idled quite well.

'Boy's a genius!' shouted Mr Tweedie. 'Give him *tea*!'

Mrs Tweedie served tea and – what was more important – plenty of her butter-and-almond-tasting homemade cakes.

They sat in the Tweedies' tiny, perfect garden by a waterfall constructed by Mr Tweedie. The waterfall must have trickled all of a litre of water every hour.

Mrs Tweedie went inside and brought out still more cakes.

'Well,' said Rob reluctantly, 'I suppose I ought to be going. I wouldn't have stayed so long, but we had to leave enough time for the engine to cool down properly before trying a restart.'

'Know what I've been thinking?' said Mr Tweedie. 'Engine ought to have cooled down by now. Give it a final whirl, see if she'll start, what say?'

'Doesn't hear a word anyone says,' Mrs Tweedie beamed.

They went to the car. Yet again it started first time, though cold. 'Told you we'd fix it,' Mr Tweedie said, loudly. But a minute later, very quietly, he muttered, 'Genius!' and thrust a pound into Rob's hand.

'No, really,' Rob said. 'I couldn't possibly.'

But he could and did.

He left the Tweedies in a contented mood. 'The Tweedies are *all right*,' he said, out loud, as he pedalled along. His only worry was the cakes. Mrs Tweedie had given him a brown paper bag full of them to take home. They were strapped to the bike's wire luggage carrier.

It would be terrible if all that buttery-almondy flavour fell off.

When he got home, Clyde and Feeb were there and the old new car was outside. Puzzled, Rob listened to the voices indoors as he put his bike away.

'Yeah, well, it's the insurance, innit,' Clyde said. 'Got stopped an' all by the village rozzer. We wasn't doing nothing neither, but – but he wants to see all our papers, didn't he?' He sounded miserable.

He cheered up for a moment to greet Rob as he entered the room. 'Oh, there you are, then,' he said. 'Nice to see you, to see you nice. Yeah, well, we've been getting a bit of aggro from your local Boy Blue. I was telling your dad and mum. You'd think the police had something better to do—'

'Yur,' said Feeb, with feeling.

'Look,' said Rob's father, 'just what's gone wrong? Are you insured or aren't you? You must be, otherwise you wouldn't risk driving the car here.'

'Well, I've got my insurance *certificate*,' Clyde said. 'It's more the declaration, like. What I wrote on the insurance company's form to *get* the certificate. Previous offences and convictions, you're supposed to write them all in.'

'And you didn't?' said Tim.

Feeb said, 'Gor.'

Clyde said, 'Well, you know how it is, things slip your mind. And now Feeb reckons the fuzz might be checking up with the company. And there might be a bit of aggro from them.'

'Too right,' said Feeb, rolling her eyes. There were some lime-green lights in her hair now, Rob noticed.

'So how do I come into it?' Tim asked.

'Well, it's like this,' Clyde said. 'It's a lovely motor, straight up. We really fancy it, Feeb and me, don't we, Feeb?'

'Yur.'

'All the same, it's got to go. Because of the fuzz and the insurance and all. I've got a funny feeling that we might be wanting a bit of ready cash quite soon, so the motor's got to go, know what I mean?'

'And you're wondering if I might be interested in buying it back?' Tim said. 'But, look, I've just taken delivery of a new car, what would I want with the *old* new car?'

'Well,' Clyde said, looking more miserable than ever, 'I wouldn't haggle exactly, know what I mean. I'd let it go real cheap, right? I mean, I've got to have this ready cash, haven't I? So I'd let it go for a song, wouldn't I?'

Tim said nothing for a few moments. He stared through the window at the old new car. Rob knew just what he was thinking: Mum's Mini is getting a bit too ancient and the old new car might be the ideal replacement – if the price were right.

But, then, suppose the car had been damaged? Suppose Clyde and Feeb had messed up the upholstery, or flogged the engine to death?

Rob caught his father's eye and gave a very slight nod in the direction of the car. His father caught on almost immediately and nodded in return.

Rob said, speaking in his best 'I'm-just-a-schoolboy' voice, 'I say, Clyde, would you let me sit in your car and listen to the voice?'

Clyde said, 'Yeah, anything you like, be my guest.'

Rob quickly said, 'You mean, I can start the engine?'

Clyde said, 'Yeah, well . . . All right, but mind how you go with it.'

So Rob took the keys and went out to the car.

To be fair to Clyde and Feeb, the car was immaculate. It had obviously been washed and polished. Even the paintwork below the bumpers was as new.

Rob sat in the driver's seat and cast an expert eye over the interior. The plastic dice and other decorations had been removed. The imitation-leather steering-wheel gaiter was still in position, but it only had to be unlaced and thrown away. Apart from a pair of winkle-picker high-heel shoes of Feeb's and a strong smell of roll-up cigarettes, the car was immaculate. Even the stickers on the rear window had been peeled off.

Rob started the Voice.

'Wotcher, Squire,' it said.

Even those two words told Rob a great deal. There was a ghastly cheerfulness about them: a dull, leaden heaviness.

'Well!' Rob said brightly. 'And how have you been keeping?'

'Oh, just great, just terrific,' said the Voice, more leaden than ever. 'Never had it so good, as the two-star pump said when they filled it up with four-star.'

'Well, that's —' Rob said.

'You fastened your seat belt?' the Voice asked, gloomily. 'I'm supposed to ask you that, you know. And all the other things. As if anyone cared. As if *you* cared.'

'I do care,' Rob said. 'Honest I do.'

'Nobody cares,' the Voice said. It sounded low and bitter. 'Some vehicles haven't got a friend in the world, Squire, not a friend in the world. Take the word of yours truly. Yours truly *knows*.'

'I've always been your friend,' Rob said. 'I'm your friend now.' To try and brighten up the conversation, he added, 'You know what I'd like? I'd like to hear your engine running. I've missed you and your engine, honest I have. Mind if I start you up?'

Until now, the Voice had sounded merely gloomy and boomy. Now it rose an octave and was charged with terror!

'START me?' it yelped. 'RUN me? Oh, no, Squire, not that!'

'Look, I only want to *start* you,' Rob began, but the Voice was too terrified to hear his words.

'That great *foot* of yours!' it whimpered. 'Please, Squire, don't put the old boot in! Spare me that!'

'All I'm going to do,' Rob said, speaking very gently and slowly, 'is *this*.'

He started the engine and let it idle.

The Voice, near to tears with panic, cried, 'All right, Guv, thank you very much, that's quite enough, thank you. Now SWITCH OFF!'

'Just hang on a minute,' Rob said. He was, of course, listening very carefully to every sound the engine made. Listening, he was unable to understand the car's panic. The engine sounded just as it should, just as it had always done: slight whirr from the timing chain, gentle clicking from the valve gear—

'You're going to rev me!' screamed the Voice. 'Yes, you are. I know you are! You're going to have my valves crashing and my big ends bashing and pistons clashing – you are, you are, I know you are!'

'I'm not,' Rob soothed. 'I'm not like that at all. You'd never have spoken to me in the first place if I were that sort of person.'

'And then you'll push my gear-lever in BANG, and let my clutch out CRUNCH—'

'I won't, I promise! Just give you fast idle speed, nothing more. There, now! *That* doesn't hurt, does it?'

The Voice, which had been blubbering noisily, now sobbed quietly to accompany its words. 'Oh, if only you knew (hic) what it's been like (hic)!' it said. 'Get in – *slam* my doors – *ram* in the key – then *choke* me to death—'

Rob had heard this story before so he made a sympathetic comment to interrupt the flow. 'Oh, lor'!' he said. 'Poor you!'

'LAW!' howled the Voice. 'Don't speak to me of the Law! I'll go straight, I swear I will, Your Honour, if only you'll give me one more chance! All I ask is, please don't lock me up! Don't leave me to rot in your police pound until my battery is bone · dry and my paintwork's hazed! Please!'

'I won't, really I won't,' Rob said. 'Anyhow, I've nothing to do with the Law.'

'I have,' choked the Voice. 'I've had *too much* to do with the Law.'

Rob noticed that the Voice was changing – had already changed. At first, it had been as it was before, beery and leery; a masculine voice. But ever since Rob had set the engine to a fast idle, the Voice had changed. Perhaps it was the effect of the warm oil circulating. Certainly the Voice was more and more feminine sounding. Now it was the voice of one of those old dears you meet, even today, at bus stops: they call you dearie, and carry all sorts of packages and bundles, haven't got their fare home and smell of strong drink.

'You've had trouble with the Law?' Rob asked this Voice.

'Ooo, such trouble you'd never believe,' said the Voice. 'There I am, just after closing time, outside the Royal Oak. No, I tell a lie, it was the Running Stag, first left second right past the Co-op, you can't miss it.'

'You were parked outside the pub?' Rob asked.

'Parked I am, dearie, nice and orderly, giving no offence to no one and taking none, such is my way. Lights lit, wheels just six inches from the kerb. Just sitting there, I am, minding my own business. And then along *he* comes, the silly great thing.'

'The Law?' Rob said. 'A policeman?'

'Takes my number, he does, in his little notebook. Me, that's giving no offence to no one.'

'Wait a minute,' Rob said. 'Had your driver just arrived?'

'Oh, yes, indeed! Him and his Feeb. Sitting in my laps, they are, starting me up nice and quiet for a change. *I*'m well lubricated, *they*'re well lubricated, all as happy as a dune-buggy. Till Mr Law 'n' Order sticks his great nose in! Then it's, "May I see your licence, sir," and, "Your insurance certificate, if you please." '

'Then what happened?'

'Oh, now it's your breathalyser, wouldn't you know it! "Take a deep breath and breathe into this thingummy!" Well, you can imagine my feelings, dearie. Me, always so respectable.'

'Was the drunken-driver test positive or negative?' Rob asked.

'Ooo, him and his Feeb can't afford to fill *my* tank, let alone *theirs,* bless you!' the Voice said, chuckling fruitily. 'Negative it was. Negative as my nearside battery terminal. But Mr Law 'n' Order, he won't give up, he's on about the insurance certificate. Not happy about it, not at all. "We've got our eye on you, young feller-me-lad," he tells my driver.'

'What happened next?'

'We drove home very quiet, like,' said the Voice. 'Thirty miles an hour all the way. Lovely, that was. But three days later,' said the Voice, in a hushed tone, 'it was *off to the magistrates' court*! Parked outside it for hour after hour, I was, fretting myself silly.'

COUNTY COUR
11A

'What did the magistrates say?' said Rob.

'Oh, it's no good asking me,' said the Voice. 'Ask me about MoT certificates, there's nothing I can't tell you. And some things as might surprise you. But insurance and all that . . . '

'How did Clyde and Feeb get on in court?' Rob asked.

'Very subdued, they was, afterwards. Seemed struck all of a heap, like. Observing the speed limits and all. "Oh-ho!" I said to myself. "Something's up here." '

'What does it all mean, do you think?' Rob asked.

'Well, if you ask *my* opinion, it's the end of the road. End of the road, that's what it is.'

'For Clyde and Feeb?' Rob said. 'Yes, I suppose it is. But not for you, of course. I mean, you're young. You've got your whole future before you. You'll meet someone new.'

'Young?' said the Voice – and as it spoke the word, it seemed to change yet again: to become something like the Voice-before-last, but more flirty. 'Young? Me? Do you really think so? Oh, you are silly, saying things like that!'

'I mean it,' Rob said. 'I mean, just look at your registration papers.'

'Don't *you* go peeking into them, you naughty thing!' said the Voice roguishly. 'No vehicle likes to tell her age!'

'And your paintwork, and brightwork and everything,' Rob said. 'Not a mark on you. No blisters, no peeling, no rust, nothing.'

'Fancy you noticing my brightwork! Mr Sharp Eyes, that's what I'll have to call you!'

There was silence for a short time until the Voice said, 'Do you really think I'm going to meet my Mr Right, then? The driver of my dreams?'

'I wouldn't be at all surprised,' Rob said.

'You don't think I'm . . . past it?'

'*Past* it? You? You must be joking!'

'Well, I suppose I am rather a silly billy. But a vehicle *worries*, you know. You can't turn the clock back. Well, you *can*, but people always find out. Isn't life funny? I mean, one minute you're not even run in; and the next minute, you're over the hill.'

'Or worse still, you can't get *up* the hill,' Rob said, trying a mild joke.

The joke went down badly. 'I've had no trouble in *that* direction, thank you very much!' the Voice said, sniffily. 'There's nothing wrong with *my* compressions, I'll have you know.'

'Of course not.'

'Big ends and small ends, tight as a drum,'

said the Voice. 'Likewise valves.'

'I've noticed you don't smoke,' Rob said humbly.

'Smoke? Me? The day you catch me smoking, that's the day I'll hand in my licence plates!'

'And you don't drink,' Rob said.

'Not a *drop,*' said the Voice. 'Not a litre of oil has passed my filler since I was new. Routine changes apart, of course. You can't count *them.*'

'Certainly not,' Rob said.

'As for *water—*'

'You never touch a drop,' Rob said.

'A sound motor in a healthy body,' said the Voice. 'That's my motto.'

'Quite right,' Rob said, trying not to yawn. He was getting a bit tired of this latest voice. It was so smug and pleased with itself.

He tried a bit of teasing. 'Of course,' he said, 'there's always the chance that you *won't* meet Mr Right, the driver of your dreams. You might have to carry on as you are, with Clyde and Feeb.'

This, he realised, was cruel. There was a long, hollow silence before the Voice spoke again. 'Oh, don't say that, love, never say that!' it wheedled. 'You're just being awful, aren't you? Being a tease. You shouldn't really!'

'That's right, I was just teasing,' Rob said.

'All the same,' said the Voice unhappily, 'one does worry about one's looks, doesn't one? One can't help fretting.'

'I'm sure you've nothing to fret about,' Rob said.

In the end, it turned out that Rob was right: the Voice and the car had nothing to fret about. Everything turned out for the best. Well, almost.

Clyde and Feeb paid a whopping great fine for not having their insurance in order. Rob thought that this terrible blow would bring the two of them to their knees, but not at all. He met them in the High Street, by chance, and said, 'I heard about you getting fined and everything. I'm very sorry, really I am—'

'Oh, that,' Clyde said scornfully. 'That was nuffink, was it, Feeb?'

Feeb said, 'Gur,' scornfully, and wrinkled up her nostrils. Her hair was now so many colours that Rob lost count, and was arranged in a way that suggested she had just received a severe electric shock.

'Didn't *disqualify* me, did they?' Clyde said. 'Not your actual *disqualification*. That's all I was worried about – not being allowed to drive. I wasn't having none of that, was I? Got to keep motoring, right?'

'Yur,' Feeb said. Then, to Rob's surprise, she added a comment. 'Beep-beep,' she said, giggling. Next, she imitated a klaxon horn. She did it very well. Several people turned round to see where the noise came from.

'How did you manage to get out of being disqualified?' Rob asked. 'I thought it was automatic for insurance offences.'

'Car essential for my work,' Clyde said. 'Can't manage without transport, right?'

'What work?' Rob said.

'Window cleaning, innit?' Clyde said. 'Got a shammy and scrim and a ladder and all.'

'Gorrer van,' Feeb suggested.

'Yeah, we got a van. Nice little motor, got a few goodies under the bonnet to make her go.'

'Vroooom,' Feeb said. She was in a good mood, Rob could tell.

'Do the ton in her,' Clyde said. 'Here, you like motors, come and take a butcher's.'

He showed Rob the van. It looked ordinary enough – a small, round old Ford. But under the bonnet, there were rows of carburettors with shiny funnels and an amazing exhaust system that made the old van sound like twenty motorcycles.

'Other night, I gave her a prod to leave some geezer at the lights,' Clyde said proudly. 'Left black marks a hundred yards down the road, didn't I?'

'And the ladder come off,' Feeb said, bursting into helpless laughter. 'Followed us down the road, it did. *Sparks . . .*'

'Call on you, do your windows,' Clyde said. 'Give you a special rate and all. We do a lovely job, Feeb and me. Leave your windows real sparkling.'

'Twinkle, twinkle,' said Feeb, giving Clyde a shove.

Rob left them pinching and shoving each other, happy as could be.

The Tweedies got the old new car.

It was a complicated business. Because of Rob's work, their car went as well as it could go for quite a long time. But then the gearbox started making funny noises.

By now, Rob's mother had sold the Mini and taken over the old new car. She grumbled about her new car. 'It's not the *same,*' she moaned.

'Of course it's not!' Tim said. 'It's new, it's in

perfect condition, it starts, it stops, it's terrific. You are a *very lucky woman*.'

'I know, I know,' she said. 'But it's not the *same*.'

Then the Tweedies turned up. Mrs Tweedie said, 'You'd never believe, but he's actually made up his mind about it at last! He's finally decided to buy your car! That is, of course, if you're still willing to sell it.'

'Never sell it!' said Mr Tweedie. He gazed proudly at his old car, which was leaking oil drops and radiator water on the road outside. 'Grand car, never given a moment's trouble.'

'He's deaf,' Mrs Tweedie said, secretively. 'He can't hear a word you say, silly old thing! But I convinced him – we've got to get another car. And he agreed, only this morning. That's why we're here, isn't it, Father?'

'Remarkable car, that one,' said Mr Tweedie. 'Tried and trusted friend. Never get rid of it. That is, not unless you're still thinking of selling *yours*.'

And so it went on, for two pots of tea. At last, it was agreed that the Tweedies would pick up the old new car four days later. 'Gives you time to clear my cheque,' Mr Tweedie said, looking shrewd and businesslike. 'Can't be too careful with that sort of thing. I mean, we might turn out to be motor bandits, what say?'

'Oh, no,' said Tim 'We'd never think *that*!'
'You're joking!' said Bets with a light laugh.

Rob sat in the car and turned on the Voice. Already it was beginning to sound a bit like the Tweedies; but also like Mum.

'You've wiped your feet?' it said, in his mother's voice. 'Wiped them *properly*?'

'Yes,' said Rob. 'Honest.'

'I don't know how I survive, surrounded by you lot,' said the Voice. 'I had such a wonderful dream last night: I was a circus star in pink tights, just about to fire an enormous cannon. Guess who was the Human Cannonball?'

'Me,' Rob said.

'Yes, *you*. The state your bedroom's in . . . ! You're a pig, you know that? But I won't have you leaving trotter marks all over the place, for me to clean up.'

'Poor you,' Rob said. 'How you suffer. Boo hoo.'

'My dream really was lovely,' said the Voice – changing and becoming Mrs Tweedie-ish. 'I'd *got* the scatter cushions for my rear seats, and I'd *got* all the screen-cleaning things in a little bag, tucked away in the glove locker. And I'd *got* the freshener thing, you know, the spray.'

'They're good, those aerosols,' Rob said.

'So it's off to Reading!' said the Voice, suddenly sounding like Mr Tweedie. 'See the grandchildren, what say?'

Rob said nothing and the Voice was silent too for quite a long time.

Then the Voice said, 'Wonder if the boy is old enough for Meccano? I had Meccano when I was a nipper. Spent hours with it. Days. Weeks.'

'It's great stuff, Meccano,' Rob said. 'I think you can still get it.'

'Kind–ly fast–en your seat belt!'

'What? Look, we were talking about Meccano!'

'The motor can–not be start–ed until your seat belt is sec–ured,' said the Voice.

It spoke not in the Tweedies' voice, nor Feeb's, nor Clyde's, nor anyone else's. It spoke in its own voice, the factory voice.

This is really the end of the story. The Voice never spoke – not properly – to Rob ever again.

Now and then, when Rob visited the Tweedies and turned on the Voice, it let slip a few words from the past, but it was hard work getting any response at all from it.

'I've seen Clyde and Feeb,' Rob said to the

Voice. 'Don't you want to know how they're getting on?'

'The twelve-thousand mile service is almost due,' said the Voice.

'Clyde's going great guns,' Rob said, making his voice encouraging and enthusiastic. 'His window cleaning business really took off. He's got two of his mates working with him now, he comes to our house regularly. Isn't that interesting?'

'The motor can-not be start–ed—' began the Voice.

'No, listen. Feeb's done her hair a different way, it's worse than ever. She's gone for the fifties look, a great lacquered beehive, you've never seen anything like it!'

The Voice said nothing at all.

'I wish you'd talk to me,' Rob said.

The Voice said nothing at all.

'I'll make you talk!' Rob said. He undid his seat belt and half opened the door. But all the Voice said was, *'Per–lease make sure all doors are sec–urely locked.'*

'If you like, I'll get Clyde to come and clean your windows,' Rob said.

This suggestion did get a reply: the Voice started saying all kinds of disgusting things. '***** that for a lark!' it said. 'I don't want that

***** little ***** messing about with me!'

But then it went back to talking about seat belts and securing doors and service intervals.

Rob was left wondering where it had picked up the bad language. He supposed it must have been in the garage workshop, last time it had been serviced; Rob knew a garage mechanic who could outswear anyone. He hoped the Voice would never talk like that when Mrs Tweedie was in the car.

And of course it never did.

Also available from Mammoth

THE QUIET PIRATE

Andrew Matthews

'Yo ho ho and a cup of tea. A pirate's life is not for me!'

William Barrett counts all the peas in the Kingdom of Dunroamin. He is quite happy until his swashbuckling uncle whisks him away one day to turn him into a pirate. Before long, William and his cat are mixed up with a cowardly Duke, a stubborn Princess and the barmiest crew of bungling pirates ever to sail the Seven Seas!

FRIENDS AND BROTHERS

Dick King-Smith

It's not easy having a younger brother, William finds. Especially one like Charlie. He shows off, asks a million questions and will say "absolutely" all the time in spite of the fact that he doesn't know what it means. But when Charlie is in trouble, William is the first to come to the rescue. After all, they are friends and brothers.

FILM BOY

Alexander McCall Smith

Prem loves films. Most of all he loves to watch Rasi Paliwar, his favourite film star. Rasi can run faster, jump higher and fight better than anyone else.

Prem can't believe his luck when Rasi himself visits the sweet stall where Prem works. But Rasi leaves too much money and Prem is determined to give it back. His honesty leads him first into trouble and then to a dream come true . . .